LUCY's BLUE DAY

This book is dedicated to:

All of my girls:
Lisa, Alyssa, Summer, Erica and Mya,
who have helped me through my own "Blue Days".

Every single person who donated to the campaign or helped getting the word out there,
whether through GoFundMe, Social Media, directly or other means.

To *Fred* & *Lesley Higgins*, my guardian angels, who, without their generosity,
this book would never have been possible.

And finally, to the people of Forfar…

THANK YOU

ISBN: 9781790586721

The right of Chris Duke to be identified as the author and Federica Bartolini as the illustrator
of this work has been asserted in accordance with the Copyright, Designs and Patents Act 1988.

Printed in Forfar by Astute Scotland Ltd

This book belongs to:

_____

_____

Lucy Pear has wonderful hair
It changes colour like no other

When the sun shines bright
and things seem right,
her *HAIR* is as *YELLOW*
as that big bright light.

When her little brother, Brad,
makes her really, really, mad,
her hair goes as RED
as her redhead dad.

One day her friend
got a brand-new toy
her hair went
GREEN with envy
no sign of joy.

When Lucy's excited,
full of happiness and glee,
her hair goes bright PURPLE
for everyone to see.

But one day she woke and the sun wasn't so bright:
she didn't feel happy, she didn't feel right.

LUCY DIDN'T KNOW WHERE TO LOOK

AND SHE DIDN'T KNOW WHAT TO DO

BECAUSE THAT MORNING SHE WOKE

AND HER HAIR WAS DARK BLUE

She didn't know why she felt so
sad, why her hair was so
blue, why she didn't
feel glad.

She didn't want to
leave home that day
and she wished the blue feeling
would just go away.

"WHY IS YOUR HAIR BLUE?"
her mummy asked.
But giving an answer seemed an impossible task
She didn't know why she felt so low...

...why
her hair
didn't have that bright
golden glow.

Up, and dressed, and off to school,
her classmates thought
her hair was cool.

Her teacher said
"IT'S NOT THAT BAD"

but she just couldn't say
"IT'S BECAUSE I'M SAD."

Her friends didn't get it...

"WHY ARE YOU SAD?"

"YOU'RE ALWAYS SO HAPPY"

"YOU'RE ALWAYS SO GLAD."

"I AM ALWAYS HAPPY"

...this much was true,
but she still couldn't say
why her hair was so **BLUE**.

At lunch, Lucy ate all she could consume when a sight caught her eye from across the room.

Her friend said

"LUCY, LOOK! SOMEONE LIKE YOU!"

And she looked up to see more hair so blue.

She could see he had a smile on his face;
a smile so bright no sadness could erase.

"BUT WHY?"
asked Lucy
IS YOUR HAIR SO BLUE?
DO YOU FEEL THE SADNESS
THAT I FEEL TOO?"

The boy looked at Lucy, with his bright green eyes
and knew that his next words could not be lies.

"DON'T WORRY, LUCY, IF YOUR HAIR GOES BLUE!
WE ALL HAVE DAYS LIKE THIS:
MUMS AND DADS AND TEACHERS TOO.

"IT'S IMPORTANT TO KNOW:

IT'S OK
TO BE SAD
IT'S OK
TO BE ANGRY
IT'S OK
TO BE MAD"

"AND IF YOU WAKE UP ONE DAY
AND YOUR HAIR IS BLUE,
PLEASE DON'T WORRY
BECAUSE
THAT'S
OK
TOO."

"WE ALL HAVE BLUE DAYS,
BUT IT WILL DISAPPEAR
AND YOUR BEAUTIFUL HAIR
WILL AGAIN REAPPEAR."

"TOMORROW YOU'LL WAKE
AND THE SUN WILL
SHINE BRIGHT

AND TODAY WILL FADE
LIKE A DREAM IN THE NIGHT."

That night, at home,
with her mum
and her dad,
she told them
she felt a little bit sad.

"BUT I'LL BE FINE"
she began to say
"BECAUSE IT'S OK, SOMETIMES
TO HAVE A BLUE DAY."

Today my hair is...

me

I'm feeling ANGRY
and my hair goes RED when...

← my
ANGRY
FACE

When I am feeling angry and my hair is red, I could....

1. Stop, take a deep breath and count to 10

2.

3.

4.

5.

I'm feeling JEALOUS
and my hair goes GREEN when...

Jealous face

When I am feeling jealous and my hair is green, I should....

1. think about all the good things I have in my life

2.

3.

4.

5.

I'm feeling HAPPY
and my hair goes PURPLE when...

Happy face ↘

When I am feeling happy and my hair is purple, I should....

1. remember this feeling and hold onto it for my blue days

2.

3.

4.

5.

I'm feeling **SAD** and my hair goes **BLUE** when...

my sad face ↘

When I am feeling sad and my hair is blue, I could....

1. speak to a friend or a grown up and tell them how I am feeling, and remember that these feelings are OK

2.

3.

4.

5.

Printed in Great Britain
by Amazon